Love That Never Die

CA Udit Gulati

ISBN 978-93-5610-065-7
© CA Udit Gulati 2022
Published in India 2022 by Pencil

A brand of

One Point Six Technologies Pvt. Ltd.
123, Building J2, Shram Seva Premises,
Wadala Truck Terminal, Wadala (E)
Mumbai 400037, Maharashtra, INDIA
E connect@thepencilapp.com
W www.thepencilapp.com

Author biography

I'm a Chartered Accountant by profession and writter by passion. I belong from Delhi

Being a CA I barely have for anything else in my life but everyone have some passion in their life which we would love to follow. In that sense my tried to follow my passion.

Writing is something that make me feel relax, I can pen down my thoughts, imagination, way to look life.

This is my first E-Book, Love That Never Die its fiction that let you connect with your love.

We all have different loves in our life, purest love of parents, crazy love of siblings, love of friend's, love that taught us a lesson, True Love that stays forever.

Reading this E-Book you can link yourself to anykind of love. I hope my readers will connect to it and have happy reading.

CONTENTS

Epigraph

Death leaves a heartache no one can heal,

love leaves a memory no one can steal.

Introduction

Narrator: Sometimes Destiny also cannot stop you from loving someone Unconditionally. It may separate you physically but a true lovers' soul can never stay apart.

Aayush, a young and highly paid investment banker, living in New York, USA, has a similar story who failed the destiny and proved his unconditional love for his Alia.

Flashback

Life is too busy these days in the USA. Being an investment banker is not easy, the company is paying a good amount for my role but my efforts are also not less. My journey to reach here is not that easy. At the age two, My parents left me in an orphanage. Life has never been easy for me. A single kid without parents and no one to say hello was what I feel like loneliness is till the age of five. But then something magical happened. I remember, When I was five year old, I saw a girl enter from the gate of an orphanage. She was Alia. Though, I was too small to understand what love was, but that was love at first sight. She was six year old when her parents died in a car accident and she was dumped at an orphanage by her dad's family. One day, I saw her alone, staring at the sky. I went to her and started talking with her. I was the first person who had a conversation with her not because I loved her or attracted it's like no one in the orphanage talks to me so I had a chance to make friends. And very soon we became friends. She used to cry a lot over her loss. I used to console her by giving her my T-Shirt to wipe her tears and nose but this is what we used to be. We were always like a shadow of each other. We spent our childhood together. Alia was a jolly cute girl. Everyone wanted to be friend of her. She loved to make friends in a very short span of time. The whole orphanage was her friend but Alia never left my friendship. Her proposal of friendship for others came with a conditional offer of one plus one. If anybody wanted to be friends with Alia they had to become my friend. Slowly the whole orphanage became our friend. We were like Rahul and Anjali of *kuch kuch hota hai*, always fighting, roaming, playing and always together. We were best buddies. Every teacher used to hate us because we were the chatterbox of class and all the students used to get inspired by us. Alia was a great dancer. when she performed, not only boys but girls also stared at her. I always used to wait for her behind the stage with a water bottle in hand. She was also the topper of the class and I was an average kid. Knowing she had so many qualities and I stood nowhere in front of her, she still always stood with me as a best friend. She loved her best friend. We spent our school life like this only.

Orphanages are usually upto class 12th after that you have to live on your own. The same happened with us as well. After our 12th result, the orphanage gave us farewell to leave and we had to do the same. Alia got rank 1 in the whole district so she got a scholarship for college in Delhi. On the other hand, I had no money, no scholarship and even no hope. I told her to leave for Delhi to start her new college life and I'll manage somehow but there she is. She didn't leave me alone.

She said "we'll be together no matter what the situation would be, no matter what life would be showing but I'm not going to leave you alone".

That was the moment when I fell for her first time. That day I realized A man just needs someone who always stands for him, whatever the situation may be. The one who's not going to leave him just because she's bored of him, or there is a tough time but one who stands for him in Happy times and sad times. The one who shares laughter with him and in sorrow holds his hand tightly and just says I'm here we'll fight through this. That day I knew I found my girl and it's none other than my Best Friend Alia.

Heading to Delhi is not easy for us but we did. She always dreamt to be a Chartered Accountant like her father was, so on her request and passion the orphanage admin swapped her college scholarship with her education funding. In this way, she got a flat to live in and I accompanied her like a shadow. I started doing some odd jobs for my education. With the help of her funding we got free food, living and education for her but it's more like a loan which she had to repay after she was qualified and got a job. I was pursuing my graduation from School of Open Learning, Delhi University along with some job and saving for my higher education funding and for an emergency fund of ours.

Beginning Of Life

We were in Delhi living together in a flat. Living under the same roof was not a big deal for us. We had been living like this since our childhood. I used to cook food for us because Alia didn't get any time for this. She had full day coaching then after returning home she used to revise everything which was taught in coaching, so I used to do all the housework for her. Even though I like to do these things, she loves cleanliness and I did that for her. For us, all the days used to be the same except one sunday in a month. We used to spend that day with full joy. We used to roam around famous places in Delhi, had dinner outside and had our movie night with popcorn. For that day, we used to wait the whole month. Apart from this, we stayed together but we had no fun. It was just like two silent guys under one roof.

As the years passed, with each day I was falling in love with her. Her cute little things made me crazy. I used to take care of her, serve her food after she returned from coaching. She was a lazy girl and sometimes she skipped food for studies. At that moment I used to feed her and scold her for not eating.

On which she used to laugh saying "Why should I care when you were here with me mommy" and burst out of laughter. She laughed like an animal *"ek dum raavan wali feeling aati h"* but it gave me lots of pleasure looking at her happy face.

My heart wanted to tell her loudly that Yes I love uh but I can't. Firstly it's important for her to succeed in her dream to be a CA as her father was so I decided to wait. Wait until she achieves her dream. I want to be part of her success, not a breaker in her success. If I can't be part of her struggle then I have no right to be part of her success. I would tell her about my feelings after she fulfilled her dream.

It's been 5 years since we left Orphanage. She cleared her CA level in first attempt and today is her CA Final result. We were scared a lot when she entered her roll and pin. She was not able to click submit. Her hands were shivering and so was mine. She asked me to do it for her. I collected all my courage and clicked, then I just opened my eyes and It was PASS. I shouted CA Alia CA Aia, she started crying looking at her result. Finally she was able to get fruit for her struggle. There was pride in my eyes for my girl. She looked at me saying "We did it" and she hugged me. I wanted to tell her at that moment but I didn't know if she would accept me or not. I didn't want to ruin her special day. I decided to keep shut.

It's her convocation day and I decided to propose to her after she got her degree. Same as I did, she came with her degree in her hand with a member welcome kit running toward me.

She hugged me tightly and said "I want to say something."

Me in a confused state asked "What?" I was damned scared if there was any other man in her life. If it's so, then I can't imagine myself without her for life.

She said "I love you Aayush, since when I don't know but I love you so much and I know you love me too. It reflects in your eyes but you respected my dream and waited for me, Aayush will you marry me??"

Me (Holyshit) replied "I love you too and Yes I'll marry you, if you say we can marry here itself. All we need in Fire, youtube will replace pandit ji" That was the most memorable moment for us.

She laughed and hugged me said "Idiot, I love you"

This is the most beautiful day of my life. My girl just achieved her dream and I was able to achieve mine. I was in the seventh sky and felt like dancing with fairies.

In these 5 years I completed my Graduation, Post-Graduation and I'm an Investment banker now. Being an Investment banker in India was not in scope so we decided to pursue our careers in the US. We wanted to achieve that luxurious life that we dreamt of in our childhood.

Finally the day of our wedding arrived. My childhood best friend and my only family member was going to be my wife today. Now legally she's my family. We didn't have a family but our orphanage is our only family. All our friends divided themself in bride and groom side. We married as per Indian Rituals with our orphanage family and the head of our orphanage did *kanyadaan*of Alia. He's not a biological father but he's the one who helped Alia to achieve her dream by funding her.

We're finally married. This feeling of life marrying your best friend was "The Moment" for me. We were complete now. Romance with my best friend was not what I thought of but it's happening and I love it. On her wedding night Alia said to me "Let's do something interesting in this night"

I replied "Alia came on sleep it's no time for pillow fight"

She just threw pillow on my face yelling *"Chutiya"*

I love to tease her. Then she stood facing wall I grabbed her from back and uttered in her ear "I know what you want and I got all preparation"

She looked at me with witty eyes and said "Fuck Off"

I replied "Done right now with you"

We spent our first night and that night was the conversion of our friendship to Happily married.

We both now pursued our education to settle in the US, she did CPA and I did CFA to pursue our life in the US.

Turning Point

We settled in New York, USA. We both started working for big corporate companies and earned a handsome sum of money.

Outside our house we're the most professional and serious person but the moment we stepped in the house, child in us wake up and we become the most idiotic person's. We used to have great time together full of life, now life is perfect mix of teasing, romance, sex, anger, and its all the mood version of Alia. My mood depends on her because the boss is always right and she's the boss of this house. I hung a poster of her on the front door written Welcome Home Boss.

I used to tease her, irritate her and she had a bad habit of saying *"agr mai mar gyi na to kya karega tu"*and I'm like I'll kill you if you utter these words again. She even loves to irritate me, that's why she used to say this again and again. But I didn't like it. I'm somehow superstitious person who believe in *'Din m ek baar maa saraswati juban p bethti h to pure din m boli hui ek baat to sach ho sakti h'*Typical Indian mentality but I believe in this and Alia hates it. She says it's all bullshit that's why she never listens to me in this case.

Alia is a person with ambitions she wanted to pursue. She didn't like to work for someone else, doing hard work and just getting a salary in return. As per her as an employee, you let your employer earn $1 Million for which you will be paid $500K, but still we work under someone because we're scared of taking risks in our life. We are comfortable with that month end fixed Salary that's where we fail as an entrepreneur. She wanted to commence a finance company of our own. She had so many dreams in her eyes. This is what I love about her. A career oriented girl who is ambitious and wants to become a successful woman.

Our life was at its best. We got our green card for the US, we got highly paid jobs, and our own house in NY, we had cars like Audi and Mercedes, life was perfect. We were damn happy with our lives. We were doing our best to make it better and more luxurious along with enjoying living to the fullest. However, our destiny has its own plans. Our happiness didn't stay longer, or I say my destiny didn't like me being happy. Some terrible shit was about to happen for which we're not ready. we would never be or nobody would be.

Our best friend Mayra was going to marry that day. I was waiting for Alia outside the church and Alia had been late as always.

I called her and said "Babes?"

She replied "I'm on my way just buying flowers for her, it won't look good if we go without any gift. No nah! it doesn't seem good her best friends didn't bought any gift that's why I'm late, now you understand babes why I'm late" (sarcastic)

I replied "Miss Drama queen, I know you okay, you late because you stepped out late from office"

She replied "I love you babes" (laughing loudly)

I replied "I love you too idiot, now be quick"

After hanging her calls, I was checking the news around and I came to know there was a terrorist attack alert in New York. This news scared shit out of me. I don't know why but I was scared at that moment. I just wanted to see her and know she's safe.

I called her again and asked "Where are you babes?"

She replied "Look at your right, I'm right here on the opposite side of road look waving hand" (smiling)

I looked at her, she was smiling, I saw her I was relaxed she gave me a flying kiss I catched it and smiled. Then, the moment she moved the car around and started moving towards the church, suddenly, I heard a sound of bomb blast. I turned around and what I saw was that Alia's body was on the church stairs in front of me. Bomb was planted just below the manhole she was standing on. Within a second our life took a disastrous turning point. I froze there and was continuously looking at her. My girl was lying in front of me. Dead!! Whole crowd from marriage came outside hearing noise, I was lying to her body crying, trying to wake her up.

How can my girl be dead? She promised me that she would never leave me.

How could she leave me? How could she be gone without me? I tried to wake her up saying "Doll wake up Doll, I know you just tease me please don't do this I can't live without you please wake up doll". (Ambulance reached) I took her to the hospital her body was semi burned, doc took her to ICU.

Meanwhile Myra reached the hospital, she asked (scared) "Alia?" just showed her ICU she sat with me crying then

I asked her "Your marriage?"

She replied "I broke it, Sam asked me to leave alia as she's dead and marry him so I just kick his ass and leave the place"

After half an hour the doc came and said "Sorry! We can't save her she's no more"

We both broke, I had no words to say I'm still not able to digest that my girl is no more, she left me alone that day I lost my faith in God. How can he steal my family from me? Doctor just easily said to me that she is no more. How can she's no more? How can she leave me? She promised me that she will never leave me alone. We have lots of dreams to chase, now what would I do without her and why should I live without her. At that point I decided I'll not live alone I have to reunite to my love I have to commit suicide to reunite to her and no one can stop me. I had decided to commit suicide after her funeral.

It's her funeral day, everyone came grief over my loss but none actually knows what I'm suffering from there was tornado in me, fight between me and god over How can god snatch my love from me she's my family all I had was her now I'm all alone in this world no shoulder to lean on.

All I want is her back until I listen to some words about life

"Life and Death were so unpredictable. So close to each other. We existed moment to moment, never knowing who would be next to leave this world. But loved one have to live for them to fulfill their last wishes so that their soul rest in peace and always remember your dead loved one is watching you always"

These lines changed my thought process until this moment. I want to commit suicide so that I can reunite to my love, hold her again in my arms, look into her eyes to say "I Love You and I'm not gonna leave you even its heaven". But now I want to fulfill her dream, our dream of life. Fulfill each and every moment that we dreamt of in hope she's with me watching me and when I finally reunite with her, I can say proudly "I fulfilled our all responsibilities and dreams. Now can I take rest in your arms"

Narrator:_This was a life changing moment for Aayush now he had to live life for her girl and he wanted it to be best._

Life Switched

I came back home and the moment I stepped in , the only thing uttered by me was "Darling I'm home" and a poster in front with Alia's photo written "Welcome Home Boss" but this time she's not here for me she never leaves me alone even not for a single day. But now, I have to live life without her, thinking of this is making me sick more. The more I think of it, the more sick I feel. Just bought her teddy and pasted her photo on teddy's face to have a feel that she's with me. We Always see in movies and webseries that you can communicate with your loved one and see them even They are dead. But why can't I see her, talk to her? My love is not true. These types of things are just ruining my mind. I can't breathe in this house. Every corner of this home has some memories of her that I can't let go.

Staircase where she used to sit after being angry at me. I remember, How she sat on the staircase with her bubbly mouth and said *"mujhse koi pyar hi ni krta"*loudly until I came to her to pamper her.

I used to say *"me to apne bache se bht saara pyaar krta hun tbhi to main apne chote se allu k liye chocolate, ice-cream, candy laaya hun, lekin thik hai agr main aapse pyaar ni krta to yeh sab main kha leta hun"*

Then she used to jump over me shouting *"ooyyeee don't you dare to have my yummy chocolate, ice-cream and candies, you moron!!"*.I used to hug her tightly, plant a kiss on her forehead, wrap her around and let her enjoy her chocolate and ice-cream which used to eat like a kid all over her face after licking the wrapper.

I was hallucinating that Alia going in balck area and I'm screaming "Alia where are you? where have you gone?" (hallucination over). Then suddenly, I came to realise that she's gone. I can't leave this house. It's hers. She made this house our home. Leaving her alone is a big no. "I will live with her memories", my heart utters. I never had food alone, she always scolded me for being late for dinner and I used to say " Why did you wait for me? If you were hungry, you should have food. Don't wait for me."She never listened to me. She always waited for me and because of her I never had food alone. However, today I have to (in sorrow). All of a sudden, there was ring on door, I just saw its Mayra (fake smile on face accompanying food with her)

She said "I know you and alia always had food together, so I thought why shouldn't I accompany you today, we're in same grief"

I just nodded to let her in. The moment she stepped in, she suddenly stopped. she might be seeing Alia like me because this home is hers, she made it.

I asked "Can we eat now, I'm hungry"

She replied "Yes please, come sit I'll serve food on table"

I asked "May I help you?"

She replied "No No, you sit I'll serve"

We just had food together. we went back to some memories of Alia. We shared and laughed a little.

Alia is a kid by heart, sometimes she's annoying but cute at the same time.

Mayra shared a moment of the time when Alia was so angry with me that she left home and went to Mayra's house. At that moment mayra was with her tinder date having some good time. Gate knocked! it's Alia with Black currant ice cream tub in her hand with a very cute little face asking mayra "May I come in?" Mayra threw that boy out of her house. Naked that guy was! literally abusing mayra outside her's home and she throw his underwear on his face saying "Chick before Dick, fuck off now". Mayra used to listen to Alia's dramatic things with ice cream and then hug her saying "Aayush is dick , leave him". On hearing this, Alia used to get angry saying "He's dick I know but I love this dick he's my dick". Mayra makes fun of her "You Shemale" after their girls night, I visit her in the morning with chocolate in my hands and sorry in my mouth. *(This is what our fights look like)*.

After remembering this moment we both started crying a little. We both missed her. She's our family and we both lost our family. People say breakup hurts but if you lost your best friend, love, family in a single person not because they left but God snatched them and you'll never be able to listen to their voice again that is real heartbreak.

Days used to pass but not for me. It seems like time stood because I can't recover from the moment I lost her. Teddy on whose face I pasted her photo, named it Alia. I used to have dinner with teddy, sleep with it, cuddle it, and talk to it about my whole day but now my alia didn't respond. She didn't laugh at my bad jokes nor did she say "my baby" to me, when I was getting angry and frustrated. I never told her to be quiet neither in fights nor otherwise because I can't live without hearing her voice. She's my life and currently without her my life is worthless.

Mayra used to be my best buddy. Now she comes home on a daily basis to see if I'm okay or not. I like the way she cares for me. She knew without Alia I'm not able to live so she came around to check if I had food, I'm going for work, having proper sleep. We both used to sit to share some memories of Alia. We three used to hang out together. Roaming around is kinda fun. We were like three idiots, always together (haha).

Once, we all went to a pub for drinks. Alia is the one who's like "Why do you guys drink alcohol? It has bad taste, if you drink bitter things you'll be a bitter person". We used to force her for drinks and after forcing and having 3 shots of vodka she was like "Vodka is the best thing in the world, vodka! I need more vodka." This continued for 8 shots after that she's best dancer in the world. she danced like hell and after that we were one who wiped her vomit. *(After which we both were like why we offered her drink, she got drunk and removed our intoxication but still we offered her drink because she is totally free minded after getting drunk).* Deep inside I loved to care after she got drunk. When we reached home I used to lay her down on the bed and she would wrap me saying "I love you baby, and you will never leave me na?" But who knows she's the one who left me alone.

Mayra brings bourbon with her offering me a drink, saying "In memory of kiddo". That night we actually got very drunk. We were in grief and had more drinks than we can handle. After that mayra was not in a position to drive back home so I asked her to stay. I don't wanna lose my only friend because of drinking and driving. I asked to sleep in my bedroom and I'll sleep on the couch in the living room. Next morning was very hectic for us. We had a high Hangover. We took some pills and she left for her place. It's a blurry memory of last night which I remember. Mayra tried to kiss me and get closer to me but I can't remember what happened next. I woke up on the couch and she was in the bedroom so I thought it's just a blurry memory and I just ignored it.

Day passed and I prepared bucket list of Alia things she wanted to do before she died, which are

1. Adopting a cute daughter. She never wanted to have a biological child, she wanted to give a happy life to orphans like us.

2. She always wanted me to commence a consultancy firm with her i.e CA plus Investment Banker.

3. She used to visit orphanages and Old age to spend her weekends with them. Play with them. she always say "In Old age home she got parents and in orphanage she got siblings"

4. She wanted us to be successful in life, achieving heights and proudly naming our orphanage which made us capable.

5. Before retiring she wanted a place where orphans and old age homes should be together so that orphans will no longer be orphans and parents who have toxic kids who left them there will get some loving kids.

All other dreams of her are just traveling the world with me which I can't fulfill without her. I'm not that capable of traveling without her but I'll definitely fulfill this bucket list. Fulfilment of this bucket list is my sole purpose for life.

Mayra decided to accompany me for completion of the bucket list and for travelling to her favorite places. Whichever place we visit we bring something special from there in memory of Alia. I want to keep a collection of everything in her memory. Mayra and I visited many places together. We visit orphanages to meet kids. We even visited Old age homes too and gave them gifts. Everytime we visit in memory of Alia. Ask them to just give a blessing to my girl.

I have a big bucket list. So I used to keep myself busy and work dedicatedly to achieve all her dreams. I needed to be more successful and I stopped meeting or seeing mayra now because now I barely had time for anyone or anything.

Mayra still tries to meet me, talking to me as per her "We are sharing the same grief at the moment and we should meet often to let us remember her, dreaming of her". She visits daily at night for dinner but I skip that because I'm not willing to meet anyone now. But she tried and I sometimes respect her & meet her.

But all of a sudden one day Sam *(Alia's office mate)*met me. He confessed to me that Alia was cheating on me with him, I didn't believe him. I trust my girl to the fullest. Sam confessed they had sex,*(I was blank for moment but still can't believe)*so I asked "When?",

All of a sudden Sam stammered and said "umm.. 25.06.2018" *(he looks confused)*, I'm suspicious of his behaviour. I looked into the calendar on that date. We were on a movie date *(I used to add our date's photo on the calendar)*. Now I know that Sam is lying but why? Then I asked to elaborate when? how?, Sam stammered and said "I don't want to piss you more man, I just wanted to confess" and he try to left, I stopped him and said "You are lier asswhole, on 25.06.2018 we're on movie date" and I punch him and said "Don't ever try to say a word about my girl asswhole" and left

Narrator's note:*A lady entered in Sam's room and said "you can't even lie properly useless" and left.*

I reached home and was confused why the hell Sam was lying to me, what his motive would be. He barely had any connection with us; he was just a colleague. That moment was just roaming around my head. I'm not able to understand why he lied to me about my dead wife. Alia was everyone's favourite and she never did anything disrespectful to anyone. She told me each and every aspect of her day. I can't remember a thing she ever told me about doing anything disrespectful to Sam either in any way. They were in different departments and had no work connection with each other. But this wording of his about my girl is killing me, how can someone dare to say a word about my girl? I can't let any person point any finger at my girl. She's my love, my bestie and I can literally kill anyone who points any finger at my girl.

I was not able to cope up with this thought. So I catch-up with Mayra and tell her everything that happened with Sam. She was shocked too and the same question she had was "Why the hell Sam did this". Mayra did something on that day, which is different. Maybe I just feel it. she put her hands on my hand with a very pretty smile, saying "Don't worry our girl has never done anything wrong which leads to shame for us and cheating in a relationship is a sin which Alia can never do".

Listening to her, I was calm. She just said something I wanted to hear which made me relaxed. After a couple of drinks we crashed back to our homes and I sat with teddy (My Alia). I kept staring at her listing her favourite playlist and all of a sudden a voice note played its our voice note. When I proposed to her for the first time, listening to her voice made me cry. She was laughing in the voice note, I can feel that love in the voice note. I just checked my phone because I remembered sometimes mistakenly I recorded some of our calls and never deleted that voice note. I played that voice note hearing her voice laughing, crying, missing her more and more. After 1 year of her being gone I heard her that it's a blessing for me to listen to her voice. After a few hours of joy I remembered I can only hear her but can't talk to her anymore. After that I just open my bottle and start drinking whenever her grief pushes me. I just started drinking. Sometimes drinking is the only solution to make you stop crying. Her grief is killing me inside.

To get out of her grief I always work 18 hour a day to be more and more successful. Success is what my girl expects out of me and I need it for her!. On one of our hectic days one of my colleagues offered me a joint (weed). As per him this increases efficiency. I tried it. That shit is fucking good man! It not only increases efficiency but also working hours. We didn't get back to home, we work smoke drink stay in office days are getting fucking cool. I never realized that I was staying in the office for 15 days and didn't even get back home but real shit happens when I get home and Mayra is there. She's in a very bad mood. I was not picking her calls for the last 15 days. She came close to me and she smelled what I'm doing. She got very mad but after that she embarrassed me fully.

She bought Alia's frame in front saying "Alia look babes what your hubby is doing these days. He's smoking weed! thing you hate the most. He's not going to be successful for dreams you saw for him but he'll be successful in coming to you early. Congratulation babes! he's coming to you. Wow!"

Then she stares at me saying "Would you say something now?" That day I realized there is someone for whom my presence matters after Alia. I always thought my presence mattered for none but Mayra being such a good friend she wanted his friend to be alive and successful.

I didn't say a thing I was embarrassed but she slapped me hard and started crying saying "You fucking idiot! Now you're my world. Have you ever thought what would happen if you left me like Alia did? I love you damid" Listening to her I just widened my eyes then she corrected "As a best friend idiot don't be happy, you're superb man but you still love Alia and I can never come between your love"

After listening to her I calm down because I'll never stop loving my girl. She's not in this world but she lives in heart and will always do. Afterwards I just gave a smile and hugged her saying "I know bro, you respect our love and thanks for that but never feel for me"

.

She just laugh at me saying "What can I do now, man like you is hard to find these days where couple in relationship cheat on each other once happening happy couple just suddenly stop loving because of third person but here's you who still love her dead wife"

That was the moment Aayush's mind struck out. Alia is the one daring person who tried to save relationships whenever she got a chance. In a moment something more added to the bucket list.

Bucket List

Listening to Mayra about that couple made me think that these days young couples are making huge mistakes. They didn't understand the basic principle of relationship i.e. respect and trust, I remembered, once when I and Alia were on a date in a restaurant a young couple was shouting and everybody were just watching them making fun. Alia jumped into their fight and said to them "Don't fight here, go home or some peace place. These people just make fun of you, go to other places and fight"

At that moment I was like "Alia you are encouraging them to fight are you serious?"

Then she told me "Sometimes fighting is necessary, they love each other I saw in their eyes but if they fight here they'll end up breaking up that's why I told them to go home and fight there. They will fight but lastly they both end up crying and hugging each other"

At that moment I was like *"Bhai tu mhaan hai"*then she used to bow down taking praise.

In that way I decided to be a love counselor who will help before break up, listen to couples and try to give some solutions or let them give solutions on their own. Mayra decided to accompany me. We both commenced a love counseling firm which we handled usually on weekends.

Life is not that easy the way it looks to be and Aayush life is more typical than any normal person. These days people used to say money can buy happiness but Aayush happiness is Alia and no money can bring her back. His money can't buy him happiness. He found his happiness in something Alia would be happy from wherever she's watching him.

One day suddenly while having a drink, I just received a few pics from an unknown number. I saw them, they were Alia's nude pics. Looking at this I just dropped my phone. I was scared and shocked but at the same time my heart was not accepting it. Collecting all the courage I picked up the phone to try to see the pics. It was shameful but I zoomed in on that pic. It was embarrassing but after zooming in on the pic I noticed it's not Alia's body, she had a birthmark on her stomach. I just saw all the pics. All of them have the same face that of Alia but body is different in all the pics. This made me angry, I just wanted to beat the shit out of that man who dared to do this with my girl.

I played smart this time and replied to that chat "Who are you? Why did you do this to my dead wife? What will you get doing to my girl? I beg you please tell me where did you get these pics from?"

After that I called a friend of mine who's in cyber police and send him pics specifying these "pics are morphed someone is trying to disrespect Alia or trying to make me hate her"

Man on whatsapp replied with "I was with your girl mate, we used to sleep together and She can't leave you but you had a small dick she's not satisfied that's why she came to me mate"

I asked "Why did you tell me this now? she's dead"

He replied "Mate, I came to know you were struggling for her since she died as a man. I didn't like it, You were in grief for such a slut. Man to Man mate just for your information I send you these pics."

I replied "Thanks mate you're such a buddy at least you open my eyes I started hating her now, how dare she do this to me? I loved her damid!"

Meanwhile my friend figured out that I was right. These pics were morphed and he figured out the location of that unknown guy too. I went to that place with his team and grabbed that aashole. I personally beat him for calling my girl slut and didn't stop until the cop took him to another cell.

Thing I'm not able to understand is why someone wants to disgrace Alia's picture or make me hate her for such cheap things. I asked my buddy to investigate him properly to get some crucial information out of his butt.

Narrator:*a lady entered the police station for that guy with food claiming to be his wife and gave him food to eat. After a few hours the lady left, and the man started screaming until the cop took him out and he's dead. As per postmortem report he was poisoned.*

I was damn angry when came to know that he was poisoned in the jail, what the fuck is our cop is doing? We even checked the CCTV camera and we suspected that the lady who called herself his wife was the only person to give him food but she had fully covered her face with a *burkha*. How can our cop fucked up so much? They let that damid die? How can I ever find who did this? Who was that lady? These questions were annoying me.

Anyhow I just distracted myself from the moment and tried to focus more on my profession. It's been 3 years since Alia passed away. Now I'm a highly paid Investment Banker in my firm and shortly I'll start my own consultancy firm as Alia always desired. Mayra now used to stay at my place having fun drinks. She is a changed person now. Since 3 years ago she hasn't gone to any tinder date otherwise she's one who's always on these one night stands.

Finally I just started love counseling. It's just over the call for beginning. Don't know if anybody will be comfortable in person but I never expected my first case would be like this.

It was a man who just lost his wife in a car accident and it's been 6 month of her death but still he had a nightmare when a car crashed and he was spared by god taking his wife with him. He had a very cute little 5 year old girl. He didn't have courage to explain to that kid where her mom was. He used to wear his wife's dress and put a mask on his wife's face to love for her after listening to her girl name. I broke out! Her name is Alia. I just disconnected the call and felt blank. How can I ask Man to move on from his dead wife when I can't do the same but I had to do this for her little girl. Just calling him again explained to him to first gather courage for himself to accept the fact that she's gone and can't come back even wearing her dress and mask to misguide his daughter is no way.

But that man said, "I didn't did this only for her but for me too I stare at mirror it feels like she's standing in front of me"

After gathering all courage I told him "Stop doing this, your life is not just yours but also of that little girl who lost her purest love of her mother. Tell your daughter that her mother is with god now and she can see her all the time, care for her and want her to be a good girl. I know she'll scream and cry but you have to handle being her mom and dad at same time. Give her your all love and time. I can't tell you to forget your wife because you can't but you can take care of her most precious love she left for you so that when she sees both of you She can feel relaxed and proud. Brother, don't think I can't feel your pain. I lost my wife in a terrorist attack and She's only one in my life. I didn't lose only my wife but my mother, lover, bestie, partner in crime. She's all in one for me. I'm all alone now. I can feel your pain brother but You're luckier than me you have daughter Alia and she must be representative of her mother. Take care of your love. Give her all of your love. Become her mom and dad at the same time. Your wife will be proud on you"

I said all I can, but didn't expect such a reaction from that man.

He said "Can we meet you? I want to meet such a powerful personality. Thanks brother. Thanks alot you just calmed the storm in my heart. I promise to take full care of Alia and make my wife proud of us"

I replied "I'll definitely meet you brother, I would love to meet little Alia"

After hanging up the call I felt relieved. It gave me immense pleasure by calming someone's storm in their heart. Today I feel my Alia must be feeling proud of me and watching me. If you watch me remember I love you doll, tell that little Alia mother her dad is prepared to become her mother. She doesn't have to worry and most importantly I miss you doll, miss you alot.

I pictured the whole event to Mayra that happened in my first counseling session. The only word she said to me is "Proud of you man". I feel good that I did something good for any person that Alia would definitely love her man's new personality.

As I always said my life is full of manholes and I hate it but I have to face these manholes too.

One Saturday evening, Mayra and I were at my home, drinking. All of a sudden she told me Alia's wish is if ever something happened wrong with her, Mayra should be one who takes her place.

I asked for elaboration, she said Alia told her "Life is unpredictable anything can be happened anytime, if something happened to Ayush I know you (Mayra) will be with me but if something happened to me I wish that you should take my place in his life because he'll be all alone without me he had nothing left with him. I wanted you to step in my shoes in his life."

Listening to Mayra that Alia wished something like this is very uncertain. She never thought like this but I trust Mayra so I believed her and it's Alia's wish so I can't disrespect it so I just said Mayra "We can give a try, I can't promise but I'll try"

Mayra gave a calm smile but deep inside it looked like she's very happy but I thought I overthink that's why I dropped the act. She then left and I told her "We can't live together until our heart accepts the fact until then we give a try to Console our hearts for Alia's wish."

After Mayra left, deep inside my heart I'm not ready for a relationship but all I think of it as Alia's wish and just making myself ready for this. At that time I was just searching her memories where I found a letter from her. Titled "What If I Die one Day" and I was shocked that she wrote something like this.

Its written "Baby, I don't know you're alive for reading this or not but If you alive than First I know you must be in a great pain if I died without you but all I say is I love you baby I love you alot and will always do whether I'm alive or not I don't know why I'm writing this but my instincts want me to do. I want you to succeed in your life or I believe you must be successful with me or without me. If you want to have another relationship you can have I give you permission but If you don't desire the same , never do it just follow your heart because at that it must be me who's talking to you through our heart as I always said babes We are connected and we'll always be. If you're reading in our old age then take care of kiddos. I left you with my responsibilities and don't be in a rush to come to me, take your time, let me have some space, So can I hangout with some handsome ghost. On a serious note whenever you read this remember your Alia is only yours and will always remain yours. We'll reunite. I'll wait for you but come to me after completing all our responsibilities whatever age it is. Love Your Alia."

Reading her letter makes me cry. I can't believe my girl wrote something like this but say it's a coincidence or her instincts letter was dated a day before her death. After I believed everyone got a last wish to fulfill and this must be her last wish to express her feeling in a letter for me.

I'm moreover confused now Why the hell Mayra lied to me about Alia? This dilemma is killing me.I rush to Mayra's place. She was very happy seeing me at 2:00 am in midnight at her place.

She asked "What are you doing here?"

I just replied "Need some answers"

I sat looking in her eyes and told her not try to lie to me, asked her "Did Alia told you make me move on or You lied to me about Alia and don't try to lie to me"

She (stummered) replied, "What are you saying Aayush! of course, she said. Why the hell do I lie to you man?"

 I didn't just stare at her for a moment, she was silent. I just stand and about to leave.

She stopped me and said "No she didn't but I like you and I know you'll never be with me so I just lied to you for starting after you fall for me I'll definitely told you the truth"

I replied "Stay away from me, you are such a liar and don't ever try to lie to me about my Alia again. I'm not gonna cheat on her, I love her. She died with love in her heart for me. Thinking about any other girl is equivalent to cheating her for me and I'll never cheat on my girl. Did you get it?"

I just stood up and was about to leave. She again stopped me saying "You're asswhole who just stuck to his dead wife. She's gone, man spare her for god sake. Move on in your life and try me"

She got closer to me, hugging me try to kiss me saying "Try it once you'll love it"

I just pushed her away saying "I'll not kiss anybody other than my and Alia's daughter who I'll adopt. I can't kiss someone the way I do to my girl I love my girl and will never cheat on her"

I was just about to open the gate for exit. She screamed saying "Don't you want to know why Sam and another guy try to convince you that your girl is a cheater, I did so! I told them to because I wanted you to think of her as a cheater so I can heal your broken heart and become yours. See How much I love you! but you're just an idiot. You always Flopped my plan."

Listening to her I was very angry and just wanted to kill her at the moment but I left her. Sometimes silence is the biggest killer than words. I know my girl is not a cheater and I didn't need anyone's proof for the same. Now I know who Alia's culprit is.

I leave Mayra for good, just closed chapter of Mayra for lifetime. I hate liars, one who doesn't know boundaries of any relation should never be trusted. One who can't be in boundaries, will cross boundaries a day with you spoiling your existing relations and will do the same in future with some other. A person who didn't know boundaries or try to cross it should be punished with a sin. Mayra crossed the boundary and I left her. She doesn't even deserve my friendship now. She lied and disrespected my Girl, my Alia.

Time flies like nothing, as said time can heal any wound but sometimes to heal a wound you need to cover it otherwise it'll grow and can be untreatable

Wheel of Time

It's been 10 Years since I lost Alia, but I still can't get over her even today. I used to talk to her photos sharing my achievements and sorrow. She's in my heart yesterday, today, tomorrow, forever. I didn't need to see her physically. All I do is close my eyes and she's here for me.

Currently I'm a successful Investment Banker having my own firm which today is earning millions of dollars. I'm up to achieving my girl dreams of having a successful life, but still all alone no-one to celebrate my success, no-one to grief at my failure. All I had in my life was me and my Alia's photo with me. I used to talk to her, sharing with her each and every aspect of life . Sometimes I feel relaxed after talking to her but sometimes it feels like someone should be there who can reply to my shits saying "Don't worry I'm with you and we'll fight with it" but 4 year ago something happened in my life that is different.

I met someone whose name is Tanu. After so many years I looked at someone else than my Alia. She was a CA in my company and surrounded by her gave some positive vibes which I've been searching for since Alia's death. I tried to be surrounded by her for the vibes that make me feel relaxed and energetic. She seemed to be complimenting me. One side of my mind deeply wanted to know more about her but the other side made sure to be consistent to Alia and not to roam but deep down I wanted someone in my life who'll not replace my Alia either, respect her place and make her own space as a family. I still remember How Mayra wanted to replace Alia but I didn't want someone like this.

I just diversified my company by adding Love Counselling in it and It became very famous among people of every age group. I proudly say that due to counseling many breakups, divorces are avoided. Even I help many heart brokens to heal but as well said doctor never eat his own prescribed medicine, here I'm one who heal other can't heal himself.

One sudden day, Tanu requested me to let her accompany me in my love session. As per her she needs some tips about love, I allowed her so that I know what she feels about love.

That day I got a case of a guy who was cheated on by his girlfriend. Guy told me his case was "Boy is a career oriented man, who is not able to give his plenty of time to his girl. He dreams of life with her once he achieves a path in his career but the girl becomes impatient after 3 years of relationship. She started seeing another guy while in a relationship with him, she kissed another guy but expected that boy will forgive her. It's just a kiss and the boy did the same, he forgave her because he can't lose her. Boy thought everything will get fine as now girl felt guilty of her deed that means she will not repeat it. But the girl didn't stop seeing other guys even though she let me dig more in her relationship and ruined it deeply. In between all these things, the boy had his final exams and after completion of exams he came to know his girl had gone emotionally with another guy and that a third person had ruined his beautiful relationship all because of the girl's impatience. But the boy was an idiot asshole who ruined his self respect and tried hard to get a girl back in his life because he loves that girl so much that he's ready to forget all that happened. All he wants is his girl back in his life. But the girl didn't even try to save her relationship. She shamelessly told the boy that She didn't love him anymore, all promises, dreams, life they ever imagined just broke in a moment. She asked him to leave her life and spare her.

Boy leaves her for good but he can't live without her. Girl didn't think before doing this that she's snatching Boy's life from him for some random guy. Life is not as unfair as it looks. Few days later the boy 's exam results were out and he passed his final examination and he achieved what he wanted to in his life but deep inside he was lonely and he lost someone who is closest to heart. At that moment he had achieved his one dream but lost another.

Here Destiny plays its role perfectly, he met with a girl who made him feel positive after so long since he lost his girl. They started having conversations, dates and boy is having a tune with this girl. She's one he always wanted to have. A kiddo with a mature mind and professional personality but now the boy is confused. Did he fall in love again?"

Then I explained to the boy "In childhood when you broke your toy did your mother repair it or bring you a new one?"

He replied "If repairing is possible she did if not she buy new one with better features"

I replied (smilingly) "Yes, this is what life is. You tried to repair your relationship with a girl but it's not possible she didn't deserve your success because she never valued your struggle but Girl who came into your life now knows your struggle, values your profession and has the same mindset as yours. This is what destiny gave you as your mother did, Destiny snatches old broken one but gives you new ones with better features. In a normal sense, Destiny snatches the one who can't respect struggle and is not deserving of success. Cheating is not the solution to anything. Always remember once a cheater is always a cheater. That cheater didn't deserve you but one who knows struggle will always respect it and having a person in your life with the same mindset is a blessing. Don't let your blessing be away from you. Grab the opportunity to go and tell that girl about how you feel. You must feel lucky brother that destiny gives you another chance to love. Don't disappoint your destiny, go ahead, you deserve a better life. You were not the wrong person but still you tried hard and that needs a lot of patience and respect. You shouldn't waste this and be with one who understands you, loves you, respects you in equal proportion."

Boy replied, " Sir, you made me realise that I'm not wrong or selfish. I deserve a better life, I'll definitely tell her today that I too love her. Thank You sir. (He left)

After counseling I looked at Tanu, she was looking at me smiling. With a huge smile on her face she said "Ayush what you suggest you should follow, Alia will love you even more if you were happy either with someone else too" and she left.

I was staring at her back, she turned around and said "I know you look at me but never noticed that I look at you the same way you look at me"

She left with a blush on her face. Listening to her made me feel awesome. I can't believe that I'll think about someone else other than Alia but the truth is Love never dies, it just shifts. Alia is still in my heart no one can ever take her place.

Love never dies, it just shifts over to another person who gives the same level of comfort, respect, compassion that you needed to complete as a person.

Alia is and always will be in my heart but Tanu made her place and she gave me the comfort, respect, vibe that I needed the most. I want someone who can stand with me in my hard and good times. Tanu is the girl she's with me at every stage either directly or indirectly. She's been with my firm for 8 years. I remembered she was the happiest person when we got some success. On the same hand, she's always ready for late nights for work. She's become part of my struggle even without letting me know.

Today, being a love counselor, I need some counseling. But analyzing the situation in front of me I'll definitely advise a man to have a life with another girl but not to forget her partner who's not more. If a case is different in which girls cheated or were disrespectful or controlling then that's not love and no one should stop him/herself for such a person who didn't know the real meaning of love. These kinds of people make fun of love, respect, and relationships. There is no sin for such a person in life.

I finally decided to ask Tanu for a date night. I texted her, I didn't know this stuff. I was out of the flirting business for the last many years.

I texted her, "Tanu, would you like to have dinner with me?". This was just a lame way of asking a girl but luck is on me

She replied "Yes, I would love to".

This is what is different in Tanu from others. She's not like other girl's running behind fancy things, she's just a simple girl with a very cute smile.

Afterwards, we met on a date. We had candle light dinner together. We had some chit-chat, and I came to know more about her. She's a talkative girl. Once she started it's like All India Radio which is non-stop. I was just listening to her thoroughly and don't know why but I was smiling while listening to her, smiling without even blinking my eyes. At that moment I knew I'm falling in love with her more and more. I was looking at her. Once she starts talking, She just goes with the flow with a smile on her face. Moment she told me something funny, the way she laughed automatically gave me a big smile. Moment I compliment her blush on her face, her cheeks move upward, her smile widens fully with reflecting teeth, the way she tries to hide it by covering it with her hand makes me feel blessed to have such a charm in my life. She tries to explain something with such a seriousness on her face that you can't expect.

Day's passed and we spent so much time together. After such a long period of time I was happy, I again started living my life. Before her, I was just fulfilling my responsibilities that I had for Alia but now I was happy as I was with my Alia.

On a sudden day I was just talking to Alia's pic and asking her If I could propose Tanu for marriage. I used to talk to her photos, asking things, sharing things. I know the photo will not reply but I feel from inside yes or no. That day I felt yes so I decided that I'll propose to her today to become mine forever.

I called her to meet, we were in a cafe I went on my knees with ring in my hand asking her "I'm widow workaholic boring person who decided not to love but you made me to change my decision, I'm not in my 20's asking you out like this but girl who made me to fall in love again. If you feel that this boring person is worth loving then you can come along with me. Miss Tanu Sharma would you like to be the only flower in the garden of my life. I love you, adore you, respect you. I can't promise to make you happy but all I commit is I'll try not to shed tears from your beautiful eyes, I love You Will you marry me?"

At that moment I was on my knees in front of the whole cafe with a ring in my hand. My heart was beating fast and my hand was shivering. She's taking a long time to reply. I was just scared of what if she said no.

Then suddenly Tanu eyes are wet, with tears in her eyes she said "I would love to be flower in your garden, Yes I will marry you"

Then I just wore her ring, get up hug her and said "Thank God you said yes otherwise I was thinking *Aayush aj to kata tera*" (We both laughed and I kissed on her forehead)

I was going to commence a new phase of my life. I'm going to marry Tanu. She asked me who I would invite in marriage, I said (smilingly) "Just a pic of Alia, other than her I had no family or friends but now you'll be part of my family".

She replied, "We're not going to invite anyone we'll marry in church in front of Jesus, only the presence of my parents and Alia would be there".

At that moment I felt blessed to have such a girl in my life. Alia must be very happy wherever she is.

Narator Note:*After a week they got married and here Aayush just entered in a new phase of life that he never expected.*

But there is never a perfect time or place for love. It happens accidentally, in a heartbeat, in a single flashing, throbbing moment.

Punch of Light in Room full of Darkness

I and Tanu had begun a new phase of life. It felt like I gained colors in my black & white picture. Now I felt good returning home as I know there is someone who's waiting for me to have dinner together, someone who's waiting for me to share my day brief. I felt like I started living my life.

I know she's perfect for me because she changes the flowers daily under the photo of Alia that I used to do. She respects that person who's everything in my family, Tanu became a part of our family.

I used to give love counseling but now the difference is Tanu accompanies me. It gives hope to many couples who lost all hopes of their relationship. Every time I saw a person smiling, thanking me I felt like Alia's saying to me "Proud of You".

On a sudden day I got a very interesting case. There was a couple who were both equally broken once and they fell in love with each other all unexpectedly. When they started knowing each other they came to know they were almost the same, same thinking level, understanding, taste, preferences but they believe relationship tag will make their bond toxic. They wanted to keep their relationship unnamed. They are just too scared of love because of their previous toxic relationship's.

We all say never repeat past mistakes but falling in love is not a mistake. It's just sometimes we make the wrong choice of person but it doesn't mean that love is toxic. It's a person who makes relationships toxic. Falling in love is never a mistake.

First I congratulate both of them that they were blessed that they were able to find each other in a world of selfish people. In a fake world, finding someone who's just as crazy as you is is a blessing. I explain to them that relationships are not toxic, it's people who make beautiful relationships toxic. There are people who were together for more than 10 years knowing that they will not be able to marry but still together with each other these people are symbols of true love, no demands , no force , just love. On the other hand, there are people who are in long term relationships but get bored with each other and start cheating on their partner. Some other people are there who just can't respect their partners, try to control them, suffocate them with their presence. These kinds of people make relationships toxic. It's not a feeling that is toxic, it's person's who made it like this. We should try to be away from this kind of person who's making our living miserable but we should respect and welcome the person in our life who's making it beautiful. True love always comes blindly. You will not ask for it but it'll come into your life automatically without any warning and you can't deny it. How much hate you give to a love relationship because of the past but a person with true love will change the definition of love in your life.

A good relationship is when two people accept each other's past, support each other's present, and love each other enough to encourage each other's future. Don't rush for love, the perfect partner will come into your life unexpectedly. Who will encourage you to grow, who won't cling to you, who will let you go out into the world, and trust that you will come back. This is what true love is all about.

I explained to the couple that's why 1 congratulate you guyz that hopefully you found your true love. Instead of denying it because of your toxic past you should welcome it with open arms. But welcome it once your heart accepts it without any if and buts.

Couple was satisfied and clear about what to do next in their life. That's my real pleasure, watching these young couples satisfied and believing in love. That's my real professional fees from them.

After they left, Tanu asked me " who can say this workaholic investment banker is such a believer of love and makes others understand the concept of love that is just disappearing in this selfish world and I'm blessed that such a loving mindset man is mine" (saying this she kissed me on cheeks). Then I just blushed. It's been a long time since I got a kiss.

Our life is going good, we were a healthy couple. We used to be together in love counselling sessions even at work even though I'm her boss. In my firm I own 70% shares and the rest 30% is in the name of Alia. Alia's share of profit is distributed as charity to old age homes, orphanages. With her share my NGO is taking care of more than 10 orphanages and old age homes each. Even her share will be utilised to fulfill her dream of a place to combine orphanage and old age home. I asked tanu that I will give her my 35% shares and make her my partner. On listening to this, She said "Instead of making me partner increase Alia's share and so that our NGO can feed more orphanages and old age home, either save it to build Alia's dream place"

I replied (smilingly) "I love you" at that moment I felt blessed.

She replied "I love you" and hugged me.

One day we both decided to adopt a baby girl. A little Angle in our life who'll bring charm, luck, happiness in our life. We went to an orphanage,we didn't want to have a biological child, we also wanted to give parent love to one who needed it more.

Just entering the place a little girl was playing in the garden alone all of a sudden her ball came close to me. She just came closer to me asking for a ball. I saw her and I fell in love with her because she's a mini version of Alia, her looks are just similar to Alia that she had when she was her age. I asked tanu that I want to adopt her, we talked to the admin and completed the process.

After I just took her in my arms asked Tanu what will be our kiddo name?.

She said "her name will be Alia".

I was shocked and happy at the same moment, she just gave words to my feelings and at the same moment gave respect to my life. That moment I know I didn't make a mistake and neither did I betray my Alia. Her place is still there in my heart but it's Tanu who made her place in my life.

With Alia in our life a new chapter of our life began. A baby not only brings happiness in the family but also spreads love. She brings back life to our home.

Tanu tied small *payal*on her legs whenever she used to kick her legs or move that *chan chan*bring joy on my face.

I used to remember when Alia wore payal I got irritated by that *chan chan*and to tease me she used to do this more often but Today when my small alia used to do the same that made me feel happy.

I really appreciate Tanu for being in my life. I used to share Alia's memory with her but she never gets irritated or feels jealous out of this as per living memories of Alia is joy for me and she loves to see me smiling like this.

There was a time in my life when I used to smile,even though I am not happy in real. I'm trying to survive everyday even though I am tired of everything and everyone. But Tanu brought back my life. She became light in the darkness of my life.

Wait is Over

Tanu and I are living a happy married life with our little Alia. As she grew up, she started questioning about "who's the lady in the picture to whom you pray daily, is she god?"

I never understood how to answer that little kid about my Alia, that she's your dad's soulmate, first love then probably question what her mom is to me then. I just wanted to avoid such a question to which I can't answer. But Tanu never left any question of her unanswered.

Tanu replied to her "She's your Mom, but she's with god now and protecting you, watching you from the sky. You can say that she's equivalent to god to you"

Alia again questioned "But you're my mom? If she's my mom then who were you to me? And Why am I never able to meet my mom? And Why should I place her at god's position"

Young children are always full of questions, and if you leave them unanswered they'll probably try to find their answer outside and can be misled. This is what Tanu thinks regarding parenting.

She replied to her "I'll answer your questions one by one, you just sit down and listen to me"

Alia sat on chair to listen to her mum

Yes I'm your mom too, but did you know Krishan Ji also had two moms. One is *Devki Ma*, one who gave birth to her and the other is *Yashoda Ma*, one who cherished, fed and took care of him. Both love him a lot and he also loved his both mothers.

In the same you too have two mothers Alia Ma and Tanu Ma. Alia ma gave birth to you but unfortunately she died due to an accident and I cherish, feed and will take care of you. In that way you Alia ma is currently with god and she's watching you, cherishing you with a lot of love. Whenever you feel alone, or need someone, when nobody is around, remember your Alia mom is there for you and you'll be under guidance always." Tanu asked our little daughter, "Alia, tell me, have you ever seen god?"

She replied "No, I never did"

Tanu replied "Then why believe god is there"

She replied "because you told me, We all are god's children we can't see him but he's there to protect us"

Tanu replied "Exactly my girl, in the same way I told you Mom is equivalent to god. You can't see Alia Maa because she's your god and you can't see her. But, she can see you. She's always watching you. So, you must be good girl otherwise your Alia Ma will scold that I'm not taking care of her little Alia"

She replied "I'll be a very good girl and my Alia mom will be very proud of me"

She ran towards Alia's photo to take her blessing and she folded her hands and whisper to Alia that "I'll be a very good girl and will make you a very proud of her maa"

At that moment I just couldn't control my emotions. I didn't know what was happening to me but I felt so happy when my little Alia uttered *"maa"* to Alia. The day I knew she must be crying too and flourishing lots of love to her little girl.

I just hug Tanu and plant kiss on her forehead saying "Thank You for being in my life"

After that day Alia never stepped outside the house without taking blessings of her Alia Maa.

As well said quote by Mae West "You only live once, but if you do it right, once is enough"

This is what I followed in my life, I started living my life with my wife and kiddo, I gave them everything I can give as a good father and husband.

Time flows like nothing, it's been 25 years since we married. Our little Alia is a 26 Year old Young Beautiful girl and it's her wedding. I was standing at Church gate as I was once waiting for my Alia to come and today I'm standing there to be the best man for my daughter in her wedding.

I was standing there and It feels like my Alia's standing in the cross road giving me a flying kiss waving hand towards me. Then suddenly I felt like that bomb blast had happened and she's lying on the stairs of church. Suddenly car horns and I'm out of hallucination, I was just scared remembering that scene.

Next I saw my little Alia step out of the car in her wedding gown, she looked just as beautiful as her mother. I as 61 year old senior citizen bend down on my knees saying "Hello beautiful, would you like to have a walk with me with I took you to your soulmate"

She replied "I'll obliged if my Superman would lead me to my soulmate"

We stepped in the church, I just give her hand to Rahul (Man she love) and said to him "I'm giving you hand of my little princess treat her well and never let her down"

He replied, "Don't worry dad, your little princess will be my Queen now and I'll always treat her and care for her as you did"

I just smiled and handed her to him.

Father started wedding rituals. Alia stopped father and said "Wait everyone is not here"

I asked "Who's missing, we all are here"

She said "look at your back"

Its Alia Photo Frame on a moving desk with gown on it, man just kept that beside me

Alia said "Now it's perfect my dad and my both mum are present in my wedding"

I just replied "Proud of you girl"

I and Tanu look at each other and realize that our parenting makes us proud today. Alia never died; she lived in all of our hearts forever.

Alia is married now, our house now feels so lonely without our little doll. But we're still happy that at least we know she's in good hands now.

I spent my life in fulfilling each and every responsibility that I inherited from Alia,

1. Today I'm a successful Investment Banker with my firm to be ranked in top 10 in US

2. I build a Place where old age home combined with Orphanage and we named it "Swarg"

3. I run a NGO in the name of Alia which is inherited my Little Alia now, NGO work on upliftment and betterment of Children's

4. I made our daughter to be successful in her life and now she handles the Firm with her life partner Rahul

5. My Firm 40% profit is dedicated to NGO (Alia) which take care expenses of Swarg and other children n senior citizens who need help

I and Tanu had a conversation and I told her, "I think I had fulfilled my responsibilities with full care and now I can rest."

Tanu replied "Yes you did, you Fulfill Alia's bucket list even you followed her kindness by being such a great love counselor, you helped and avoid many break-up n divorce, you make people believe in love again. You did a great job, Alia must be so proud to have love in her life"

I replied "Thank you, I'm also very proud to have partner like you in my life who not supported me in every phase but also gave my Alia that respect n honor that I gave, I Love You"

She replied "I Love You, Alia's our family giving her respect and honor is my duty" (she smiled)

I just received a call for counseling in a restaurant

I asked Tanu "Work Call ! , Should I leave?"

She replied "Work first, someone need your help go for it"

I just stepped outside the house and all of sudden I Came in and hugged Tanu and kissed her on the forehead and said "See you."

She asked "What happened to you all of a sudden?"

I replied "I didn't know, it's just feel like I want to hug and kiss you and so I did"

She laughed and said "See You Soon"

I left home for a restaurant, I was waiting for my client to show but he didn't. While I was waiting I saw a couple fighting in the restaurant and I felt like the moment it all started. The moment, couple fought in the restaurant, Alia consoled them and advised them. I got inspiration to do the same.

Suddenly, I saw that the girl was making her face look like a puppy and the boy said to her "Don't do this! I just totally tired from you" and about to leave

I just stood up went to that boy and asked him "How are you brother"

He recognised me, he said "Are you Aayush the famous Love Counselor"

I replied "I didn't knew that I had such popularity among youngsters"

He replied "Sir, we used to listen your podcast and we love you the way you explain is Just awesome"

I replied "Thank you so much for such appreciation but can I talk to you for a minute"

He replied "Yes please, I'll be honoured"

I replied "I'm just trying to stop you from doing your greatest sin of all time, girl sitting there, look at her. I was observing you, you shouted at her and she made a cute puppy face. I understand there must be some issue between both you but she loves you a lot, she's still sitting there crying. If she didn't love you she might stand and kick your ass and step out of this restaurant but she made a puppy face to calm you down. You know, this puppy face is so special in a boy's life, having someone who tries to calm your anger down is blessed in this selfish and cruel world. Don't lose her over any argument, go back to her, hug her, kiss her, say sorry. Any kind of issue can be resolved by discussion without being angry. Sometimes arguments are also necessary in a relationship but in such an argument where seeing one angry other calm down is called bond. You have such a beautiful bond, now go and grab your girl. Always remember never let your girl cry over you, be her strength.

He replied "Thank you sir, you just stopped me from losing my precious gem of life"

Boy run back apologise her in front of whole restaurant, propose her bending on knees then hug her and they look so happy together.

Aayush just saw them, gave a smile and left.

But he didn't know what's standing next for him, he just stepped in his car and all of a sudden a rush truck at speed of 180 kmps came from behind and crashed the car. At that moment Aayush lost his breath.

Nothing, they say, is more certain than death, and nothing more uncertain than the time of dying.

He never knew his time for reuniting with Alia is the moment from where got his inspiration of being a Love Counselor.

Alia must be waiting for her Aayush and when they finally United, Aayush can proudly say to her "Yes I did, I didn't run as coward I Fulfill our responsibility and lived a happy life but now I'm tired just wanted to sleep on your lap as cushion"